For Diana,
We really did grow up to be artists.

Follow and Do
Confession

Written and Illustrated by Joni Walker

CONCORDIA PUBLISHING HOUSE • SAINT LOUIS

Dear Parents,

Confession, and the Office of the Keys, is the "doing" behind what we pray in the Lord's Prayer: "forgive us our trespasses as we forgive those who trespass against us."

We are to CONFESS our sin against our neighbor. We are also to forgive our neighbor who sins against us. Parents model this with and for their children. Not only should children learn to say "I'm sorry" when they do something wrong, but parents should learn to respond with "you are forgiven." To respond with a simple, "it's okay," misses the freedom that forgiveness brings.

"Forgiven" means two things. First, you are no longer guilty, which means, second, the wronged person no longer has anything to hold against you. A child who is consistently forgiven is all the more aware of the gifts of his Baptism, the washing & renewal.

The second aspect comes in the Office of the Keys where we

acknowledge (confess) that all our wrongs are sins, ultimately, against God. In this part of the catechism, we hear that when we confess our sins to the pastor, he will speak to us the truth that God sets aside His judgment against sin, for Jesus' sake. Through the authority given by God, our pastor can extend to us the forgiveness of God.

What comfort it is for guilty consciences to hear that what God's Son did 2,000 years ago is for you right now, today. Jesus Christ died for the sins of the world, even yours, even your child's. Admitting and confessing our SINS is a difficult thing. But as Christians, we can be confident that we are forgiven in Christ and that we can forgive others.

Luther said that parents are the priests of the family. When it becomes the family's practice to confess and forgive sins, children are strengthened and learn to value confession. Then, they value even more the forgiveness that is theirs as God's own children,

What is Confession?

Confession has two parts.
First, that we confess our sins.

I am sorry for the bad things I have done.

And second, that we receive absolution, that is, forgiveness, from the pastor as from God Himself, not doubting, but firmly believing that by it our sins are forgiven before God in heaven.

I believe God forgives me.

7

What sins should we confess?

Before God we should plead guilty
of all sins, even those we are not aware of,
as we do in the Lord's Prayer;

when I ask God to forgive me, He forgives all of my sins.

I feel badly for
the way I acted today.

But before the pastor we should confess only those sins which we know and feel in our hearts.

Which are these?

Consider your place in life according to the Ten Commandments:

Are you a son, daughter, sister, brother or student?
Have you been disobedient or lazy?

I did not help my brother rake leaves today.

Have you been hot-tempered, rude or quarrelsome?

I got mad and yelled at my brother.

Have you hurt someone by your words or deed?

I made fun of a girl in my class.

Have you stolen, been negligent, wasted anything, or done any harm?

I did not take care of the book I borrowed from my friend.

Please forgive me.

Pastor, I have done bad things and ask you to hear my confession and to pronounce forgiveness in order to fulfill God's will.

Let it be done for you as you believe.
And I, by the command of our Lord Jesus Christ,
forgive you your sins in the name of the Father
and of the Son and of the Holy Spirit.

Published by Concordia Publishing House

3558 S. Jefferson Avenue, St. Louis, MO 63118-3968

1-800-325-3040 • www.cph.org

Text and illustrations copyright © 2005 Joni Walker

Manufactured in China

1 2 3 4 5 6 7 8 9 10   14 13 12 11 10 09 08 07 06 05